Born in Coventry of parents working in theatre, Josie Davies was educated at Daventry Grammar School and entered the Civil Service after the war.

She later trained as a Junior School Teacher and taught in the U.S.A. from 1957 to 1958. After gaining her LGSM and LRAM Diplomas she moved to Coventry Technical College to teach Speech and Drama.

For twenty years she worked as an actress and producer in amateur theatre and turned to writing in 1980, beginning with magazine articles and short stories. Her poetry has been published widely and broadcast on local radio.

Journey to Marble Mountain

Josie Davies

Journey to Marble Mountain

Nightingale Books

A CIP catalogue record for this title is
available from the British Library.
ISBN 978 1 907552 12 0

*Nightingale Books is an imprint of
Pegasus Elliot MacKenzie Publishers Ltd.*
www.pegasuspublishers.com

First Published in 2010

**Nightingale Books
Sheraton House Castle Park
Cambridge England**

Printed & Bound in Great Britain

To Elaine who came…
And stayed for the journey

Chapter One

Trouble in Seph

"Go and milk the stars, Azdra. And while you're about it – fetch a bucketful of wishes for your mother."

Azdra looked up from his game at the clear, blue sky where lived the Great Gom, Lord of the High.

"What stars, Father? It is broad daylight."

"I know that, you lazy boy. I only said it to wake you out of your daydreams. There are more things in life than playing games, you know. Now stir yourself and don't be late for supper." And, shaking his head sadly, the man went away into the yellow stone house he had built ten years ago for his family.

The boy squinted up at the sun through the large spectacles he had lately taken to wearing. Not that he *needed* spectacles – they were a gift given away with his packet of Whizzo Wheaties – and he thought they made him look important and clever.

In fact, they gave his thin face an owlish appearance and were always slipping to the end of his nose. This made the other boys laugh at him. But Azdra didn't mind – he preferred a puzzle to a pal any time. And he wasn't *really* lazy – he just liked to do things at his own speed.

Now he was smiling to himself. "Father thinks his riddle caught me out, but it didn't. Our two cows are named after the stars Castor and Pollux. And wishes come from a well – so, he wants me to milk the cows and fetch some water. I'll finish this game of marbles and *then* I'll be ready."

A leaf fell on to his hand as he sat on the ground. "That's funny, Leaf Fall is not due for another three months. And the ivy on the wall is looking sick for the first time in its life. Ah well." He shrugged and turned back to his favourite game.

Another leaf fell amongst the beautiful, coloured balls. Impatiently he brushed it away – and then something made him stop and listen.

Yes – there was the something again.

It was usually very quiet in the Land of Seph. Only when matters had displeased the Great Gom, was there a rumble in the air. "Yesterday there was a rumble – *and* the day before – and now, *another*," whispered Azdra, becoming more and more nervous. "What has gone wrong? Who is to blame? And he began picking up his marbles. But his fingers were all thumbs and he dropped as many as he picked up.

The sky was darker now and the trees began to sway like Old Man Zimba weaving his spells. Frightened, Azdra started to run towards the house but the wind was too strong. "I can't move," he gasped, "it's just as if I'm pushing against a wall that isn't there. Jumping Jehoshophat! What's happening now?"

A sudden gust of wind knocked him flat on his back. There was a flapping of wings and the sky above his head was filled with the great black she-bird, Bombelina, Messenger of Gom!

Azdra had heard stories about her wisdom and bravery. Once, Gom's special ear muffs, which shut out the noise of the thunder-clouds, had broken down. And Bombelina had flown many miles to fetch High Sky Engineer back from his holiday. Then the faithful bird had held two warlike clouds apart with her wings to prevent any noise, until the muffs were repaired. Aching wings saved an aching head!

And here was Azdra cringing in Bombelina's shadow, staring up into her face. His teeth were chattering and Jehoshophat, his pet jumping-bean, (Phat for short) was bouncing about in his hat and making *his* head ache.

"H-how-how do you do, your royal – er – madam..." began the boy, trying to get up. But Bombelina very gently but firmly held him down with her foot.

"The Great Gom is angry."

"Oh yes, he is, he is," agreed Azdra, nodding his head and also the bean out of his hat.

"Do not interrupt," said the bird in her deep, dark voice. "Five of the most precious stones in the Crown of Gom are missing…"

"Oh dear, I *am* sorry…"

"*And*," continued the bird, "it has come to our notice that *you*, little boy, are using one of them as a *plaything!*"

"Oh, no, Miss Bombelina, you've got it all wrong."

"We are *never* wrong. See, there it is amongst those cheap marbles. The Pink Pearl of Truth. Why did you steal it? Come to think of it – *how* did you steal it?"

As Bombelina lifted her foot, Azdra scrambled up, putting Phat back in his hat, and bowed low.

"Oh, *please*, Madam Messenger, believe me. I did not steal the pearl. It was just there… another marble, I thought."

"Ah! You just found it, did you? A fine story. And one which will not be believed by the Great Gom. As a punishment, he commands you to find and return to him the other four stones: the Diamond of Strength, the Ruby of Love, the Silver of Wisdom and the Gold of Power. Until this is done, nothing will grow in the Land of Seph." And so as if to add strength to her words, a great shower of leaves fell around the boy as Bombelina rose into the High and was gone.

"Well, here's a how d'you do!" exclaimed Azdra, pushing his spectacles back up his nose. "Not only do I have to milk the cows and fetch water, I also have to save the Land of Seph by finding Gom's treasure. What a *puzzle* that will be." And he bent down to collect his marbles.

But as he did so, the earth trembled and the glass balls ran in all directions. Azdra ran after them, and the Earth laughed and laughed until she split her sides. Great cracks appeared all round the boy until he was standing on a heaving hummock which finally broke away completely. And with shrieks of laughter ringing in his ears, Azdra felt himself falling into the darkest night he had ever known.

But all nights come to an end and then he would wake up... wouldn't he?

"Ou... ou... ch!" It *had* come to an end and a very hard end it was too. "But if the night is over, why is it still dark? And I must be wide awake after all because my head aches and my back aches and the bean is still bouncing. Jumping Jehoshophat!" wailed Azdra, peering through the gloom. "Where on earth are we now?"

Chapter Two

Riddles and Mazes

If beans could speak, Phat would have told Azdra where they were – but jumping was his only talent. So it was not until five minutes later when rough hands seized the boy that his question was answered.

"You are in the land of the Mighty Mog, Lord of the Low – come!" And Azdra was dragged along narrow, winding passages which opened up into a large cavern. At last he could see his surroundings.

The light was coming from hundreds of tiny creatures walking round and round on a shelf high up on the walls. "I say," he gasped, "caterpillars with lanterns, what a joke."

"No joke," snapped a voice from the far end of the cave, "glow-worms. They're permanently lit up – and very useful they are, too. We use them all the time here. A glow-worm a day, keeps the darkness away. Ha! That's good – very good. I like a rhyme before breakfast."

Azdra made his way carefully over the rough, stone floor littered with scraps of paper. He stepped in front of a platform on which there stood a small man with a nut-brown face. Not a single hair grew on the top of his head, but a long, white beard trailed on the ground. So long, the boy noticed, that it had to be tied into several knots.

"I am Elddireth, Master of Riddles, and this is Puzzletime." The man picked up a long pointer and prodded two tortoises standing nearby.

"You there, wake up, wake up! Put on your thinking caps and answer!" The creatures duly woke up and put on two little red caps. "What is two times two ones? Quickly, quickly!"

"Two ones are two," replied one tortoise proudly.

"And – er – two times two is four," answered the other.

"Wrong, wrong," cried the delighted Master. "Two ones, side by side, are eleven, and everybody knows two elevens are twenty-two."

"But that's not fair," began Azdra.

"Quite fair, quite fair," said Elddireth laughing, tearing up the question and throwing it onto the floor. "Now it's *your* turn. What has eight legs and likes spinning? Well? Come on, come on."

"Oh, that's easy," boasted Azdra. "I'm used to much harder puzzles. A spider – he has eight legs and likes spinning."

"Wrong, wrong. The answer, as you should well know is – four children on a round-about."

"But…"

"No time for buts. Next question. What has two eyes, is very sharp and always in stitches?" The tortoises were scratching their heads, and Azdra was thinking of his mother making clothes.

"I suppose," said Azdra, crossing his fingers for luck, "that you are talking about *two* sewing needles."

"Wrong again," shouted Elddireth, jumping up and down like a yo-yo, "I was talking about a man, who is very clever – who is always laughing. Someone – like – *myself*!"

"But that's just silly," declared the boy.

"Yes. Silly, silly," repeated the tortoises, glad they had found a friend to back them up.

"*Silly* is it?" gasped the Master. "We shall soon see about that." He pressed a button on the wall, and straight away the slabs, on which Azdra and the tortoises were standing, began to move and then sink. All three were carried slowly downwards, tipped off onto the floor and left panting while the slabs returned to their positions, blocking up the hole in the ceiling.

"Jumping Jehoshophat," sighed Azdra.

"Jumping Jehoshophat," echoed his new friends.

"We're really in a hole this time," said Azdra, searching the cave, high and low, for some means of

19

escape, "This isn't my day. I've lost my marbles. I've lost the Pink Pearl, and now I've lost my freedom."

"Lost our freedom," sighed the tortoises.

Suddenly, Phat started jumping again. One, two, three, over and ou...t. He landed on the far side of the cave. "Gosh, Phat – you'll hurt yourself," said Azdra, stooping to pick up the bean. And then he saw – an arrow, scratched on the stone wall. Then another and another. "Hey, we may be lucky yet. This is like a game in one of my books at home, where you follow the arrows to get out of trouble."

One hundred arrows later, he was still *in* trouble. Three times they had led him to a secret door which opened up into another cave. Each cave was smaller than the last and now he was sitting in the smallest cave where there were no more arrows and no more doors. "That's it," he grumbled. "I'm not playing *this* game any more."

"Any more," grumbled the tortoises.

"Great heavens. How did *you* get here so quickly?" exclaimed Azdra, leaping up and bumping his head. "Where I come from, tortoises travel slowly."

"But down here we do things differently," said the one.

"Yes, we are not tort-oises, we are fast-oises," said the other.

"I wonder," thought Azdra, always on the look out for clues, "if *differently* is the clue we're looking for. Instead of following the arrows forwards, let us be different and go backwards."

Sure enough, high in the wall above the first arrow, Azdra could feel a crack. And after much pressing and stretching and puffing and panting, a door swung inwards. The fastoises sat one on each of the boy's shoulders and Azdra climbed up and out of the cave into another world. A place of brown paths and green hedges and bright light.

"This is more like it," said Azdra, taking a deep breath.

"More like it – like it…" echoed the fastoises as their feet touched the ground and they scurried away into the greenery.

"Come on, Phat. Let's see where this path takes us."

The path smiled to itself as it took the boy round to the right, along to the left, right again, left again, forwards and back until the boy declared: "That's enough, Brown Path. You win this time, but I'll beat you yet. You won't keep us in this maze forever."

"Help, help!"

"Aha – someone else is lost. Sounds like a girl, though." Azdra didn't have much time for girls. "Still, she *might* know something useful. "Hello," he called, going in the direction of the voice.

"Hello…oo."

"Hello…oo."

"HELLO!" They bumped into each other round a particularly sharp bend. Both ended upon the ground and between them lay a tiny ball which had fallen out of the girl's hand.

"The Pink *Pearl*," whispered the boy in astonishment. He stared angrily at the girl. "Who are you? And what are you doing with my Pearl?"

Chapter Three

Domino Downs

The girl had long, black hair. It hung round her face just like thick, velvet curtains, thought Azdra, and her amber eyes made him feel very uncomfortable. She gave him a strange look when she answered his question.

"My name is Bel. As for the Pearl – it was there! I just – found it."

"Well I found it first and it really belongs to the Great Gom, Lord of the High. As a matter of fact, he has chosen me to find the other treasures from his crown." And he stooped to pick up the Pearl, but Bel was quicker and covered it with her foot.

This was too much for Azdra. He was never going to get back to Seph at this rate, and he pushed the girl away. So began a ding-dong fight between the two. Bel was strong for a girl, and they rolled over and over on the ground. Her long hair covered

Azdras's face – he made a wild grab and fell backwards as several strands came away in his hand.

Turning over and reaching for his spectacles, he was just in time to see the cause of the fight, the Pink Pearl, rolling down the path.

"Jumping Jehoshophat!" he yelled. Down the path he ran, quickly followed by Bel. But no matter how fast they moved, the Pearl was always ahead, rolling, bowling, turning and twisting through the maze.

And then suddenly, round a corner – no more hedge, no more path. Just lovely, lovely space – green fields and gently rolling hills as far as they could see – and the Pearl *stopped*. And the children *stopped*.

"Oh, boy," said Bel.

"Oh, girl," said Azdra. And they burst out laughing.

Bel picked up the Pearl. "Here – keep it safe."

"Well, Pearl, you know the way – and that's the truth," smiled Azdra as he put it in the leather bag on his back. Bel was nursing her right arm. "Hey, you've hurt yourself."

"I had a fall before we met, and that fight didn't help one little bit."

"I'm sorry," mumbled Azdra, fidgeting and looking at his feet. He wasn't used to sharing his world with anyone else. Then he looked Bel straight in the eyes and said, "Look we both want to get out of here, so, you can come along with me if you like."

"Thanks," said Bel, smiling and thinking to herself, I was going to tag along anyway!

It was a surprise to Azdra that he began to feel better – not many people had had reason to say 'thank you' to him before. He took off the red and white sash he wore round his waist and made a sling in which Bel could rest her damaged arm.

The Pearl had stopped at the foot of a signpost, and a big grin spread over Azdra's face as he saw what was written there – DOMINO DOWNS.

"Yippee!" He threw his hat in the air, making Phat feel quite sick. "I could just do with a game of dominoes. I usually play every night, back home in Seph."

"Not now," moaned Bel. "You've more important things to do."

But Azdra had made up his mind. "You can stay here and rest if you want to. I shan't be long," and he started off across the field. "I wonder where I shall find them."

"Here," came a voice behind him.

"Here," said another in front.

"Here, here, here," from the Dominoes popping up through the ground on all sides.

"And last, but not least – here!" And all the twenty-seven Dominoes turned to face their leader, Double Six, standing on the brow of a hill like an Indian Chief.

"Jumping – Je-hosh-o-phat!" gasped Azdra. "Some Dominoes! They're bigger than me." The ones he played with at home were small, oblong pieces he could hold in his hand – black with white spots. The most valuable piece had two groups of six spots – the double six – and here he was walking towards Azdra until he stood looking down on him.

"So you want a game, little boy?"

"Er – yes please, Mr Sixes. I've er – won many times at home."

"And who do you play against, clever child?"

"Why, myself of course."

"He plays against himself, of course," shouted the Dominoes, pointing at him and shrieking with laughter.

"But here, you must play against our man, Fab."

The leader thumped the ground, and out of a hole in the hillside stepped a giant of a man, covered in hair.

Azdra knew Fab would have no difficulty in handling the huge Dominoes, and guessed he was a very, very good player too. In fact, Azdra wished he was at home milking Castor and Pollux. Even fetching water from the well seemed a good idea from where he was.

Suddenly he didn't want a game of Dominoes at all.

"Er – Mr Sixes," he began. But then he noticed something odd about another piece standing opposite.

Double One was winking at him! *Was* he winking or was one of the two spots twinkling and shining in the light – sparkling – like a *diamond*? Could *this* be the Diamond of Strength? He must stay to find out. "Mr Sixes – if I win, do I get a prize?"

"Anything you ask for will be yours," declared Double Six.

"Anything?"

"Of course, of course. *But* – you won't win. Now," shouted Double Six, like a Sergeant Major on parade, "all Dominoes, face down – *fall!*" All the pieces fell to the ground so that their spots were hidden. To the players, he said, "Choose your Dominoes. Get set – g...o!"

The game began.

Sure enough Fabman *was* good and moved the pieces easily, as if they were made of paper. But poor Azdra huffed and puffed as he pushed them into place. And what is more – something very peculiar was going on. All the spots on *his* Dominoes kept changing places.

"This is hopeless," he groaned. Perhaps his spectacles wanted cleaning; but a good rub with his hanky made no difference. He either had to miss a turn or pick another Domino.

Fabman had no trouble with his pieces. They behaved beautifully and soon he had played them all. Azdra was left with a heap of good-for-nothings.

"First game to Fabman. Take a short rest," said the delighted Double Six.

The light was beginning to fade and Azdra was getting desperate. Bel would be tired of waiting, and he was no nearer winning the Diamond. "There must be some way out of this mess. If only I could think of one. Oh dear, with so much thinking, my spectacles are steaming up again."

He rummaged in his bag for the hankie, and this time he felt the packet of herbs and nuts he should have taken home to his mother for supper. "A – tish – oo!" And some pepper! "A – tish – oo!" Off popped his spectacles. "Now there's an idea," grinned Azdra.

"Take your places for the second game," commanded Double Six.

It was now or never.

Holding his nose with one hand, Azdra grabbed the pepper with the other hand and ran amongst the Dominoes. Wildly he scattered the pepper, right, left and centre, keeping the last dollop for Double One – who, as usual, was standing apart from the rest.

The fields were alive with the sound of sneezing. Sneezes echoed from hill to hill. *"A – tish – oo!"* exploded Double One. The Diamond shot from its hole, over the head of Azdra, to land in a small hollow behind him.

Turning around, Azdra let go of his nose, snatched up the Diamond – and RAN!

Chapter Four

Bull's-eye Bounce

Bel was sitting, half asleep, under a Ping Pong Tree.

"A – tish – oo!"

Bel was wide awake under a Ping Pong Tree, staring at the Diamond in Azdra's hand. "You've got it! Oh I *am* glad. You must have played very well."

"Er – not one of my *best* games, actually," he admitted, blushing. "In fact it was a terrible game – but," he added, laughing, "I put some pep into it before I finished. Let me tell you all about it."

"Not until we've eaten."

"*Eaten* – now there's a word I didn't think I'd be using again."

"Ah, well," said Bel, pleased as a cat with a saucer of cream, "while you've been amusing yourself…"

"*And* finding the Diamond," put in Azdra.

"...and finding the Diamond, *I* found an orchard. Hey Presto!" She whipped away some large leaves to reveal a feast of fruits – the funniest fruits Azdra had ever seen. There were Ping Pong Plums, Tennis Tapples, Golf Goranges, Soccerberries and a pile of nuts with even nuttier names.

They ate and they talked and they laughed.

And they slept under a Tapple Tree.

BUT NOT FOR LONG.

A whiz of air went past Azdra's nose. Bel cried out in her sleep. Azdra tried to lift his arm but couldn't. But he did open his eyes very slowly, to discover his sleeve pinned to the ground by a silver arrow. Two more pierced his trouser legs. And Bel's beautiful hair was caught by a dozen arrows arranged like the points on a silver crown.

"G-got you," squeaked a voice by Azdra's right ear.

"C-caught you," squealed a voice by his left ear.

"G-good."

"G-great."

"G-grand," squeaked a dozen voices as their owners jumped down from the trees and bounced round the children.

Bel woke up, startled, to find a rosy-cheeked Tappleman on one side and a red-haired Gorange on the other. Both were armed with bows and arrows.

"Y-you've b-been stealing our f-fruits," said a Ping Pongman.

"But you w-won't g-get away with it," said a Soccerberry.

Azdra tried to sit up but was bounced on and he fell back with a groan. "We didn't know the fruit belonged to anyone."

"You d-didn't ask, did you?"

"There was no one to ask. We're very sorry."

"S-sorry's not enough. The Annual Arrowfest is b-being held in Bull's-eye Wood. And s-so far we haven't found anyone to p-play against. You b-boy, shall have a chance to prove yourself as an archer. Only if you win, can you g-go free."

"And if I lose?"

"You b-both become the targets. H-ha, h-ho, he-hee."

Quickly, the arrows were pulled out of the ground, and the children were pushed and bounced along until they came to a large clearing in a wood.

In the middle, stood the target – a round board on which were painted coloured rings. And in the centre, forming the bull's-eye, a most beautiful stone of rich crimson tinged with purple, glowing amongst the woodland green. Bel and Azdra looked at each other. Without knowing it, their bouncing captors had led them to the third treasure – the Ruby of Love.

Two Soccerberries stood guard over Bel while Azdra was supplied with bow and arrows. Back home in Seph, Azdra was known as a good marksman and now he felt sure he could produce a high score by sending his arrows straight to the centre of the target.

But this was a long way from Seph.

And these arrows were not like any other arrows.

Azdra took aim and fired.

Number One went to the right.

Number Two flew to the left.

Number Three headed straight for the bull's-eye, then changed its mind and came back again, and so on – until the last arrow, which circled three times around the target and then fell defiantly at the boy's feet.

All the tooting fruities bounced with joy.

"This evening we will return for the Grand Arrow Feast, and you will be our Targets for T-Tonight," squeaked the largest and rosiest of the Tapples. And without more ado, the unhappy children were tied, back to back, to a tree.

"We've just got to get that Ruby and be away from here before those beastly bouncers come back," declared Azdra, struggling to be free. His hands had been tied together but because Bel had one arm in a sling, her other hand had been forgotten in the rush.

"We can only make the best of what we have," replied Bel.

"And we only have the Pearl and the Diamond."

"Exactly."

"The Pearl led us out of Mog's maze, so…"

"…the Diamond might help us out of Bull's-eye."

"Mmm," frowned Azdra. "I remember reading somewhere that diamonds are so hard they can cut through things."

"So – what are we waiting for?" cried Bel, excitedly. It was a piece of luck that *she* now wore the bag containing the jewels – handed to her while Azdra was firing his arrows. Although she had to use her left hand, it didn't seem to matter to Bel. Quickly she found the Diamond and, using it as a cutting edge, began rubbing it back and forth across the ropes.

It was a slow process, but it was working. When she was almost through the last threads, she saw a wandering Gorange bouncing their way. Bending over the cut ropes to hide them, she looked suitably frightened at his approach.

"It w-won't b-be long now," bounced the Gorange all round the tree. "Targets for Tonight. Ho ho," and he was gone.

"No, it won't be long," whispered Bel, snapping the final thread. Azdra's hands proved awkward, but as the sun began to loosen his grip on the day, the ropes lost their grip on the boy and he was free.

"Now for the Ruby."

"E – e – k, e – e – k, a – ah – k."

Azdra stopped in his tracks. "What a funny noise."

"Never mind funny noises, come on!" urged Bel.

Again there was a long creaking, "E – e –k."

And a hand caught hold of the boy's shirt. Azdra thought the Tapples had returned, but looking up, saw he had been dragged back by the branch of a tree.

"A – ck – e," moaned the tree.

"Oh – you *ache*!" said Azdra. And he could see why. Several arrows had pierced the bark and trickles of sap were running from the wounds.

"Oh, do hurry," cried Bel, pulling him towards the Ruby. "Don't waste your time, the Tapples are coming."

But Azdra was already climbing the tree and tugging at the silver shafts. He couldn't leave the poor old thing in pain, could he? As the last arrow came away, Azdra heard Bel gasp. The Ruby had fallen from its prison in the Bull's-eye. Just as if it had been waiting to see a little bit of love and kindness. It was theirs for the taking!

Now the three stones were safely tucked away in the bag. The bag was on Azdra's back once more and there was nothing else to keep them.

Or – so they thought.

But in the excitement, they had not noticed One Tapple,

Two Tapples,

36

Three Tapples, Four, bouncing quietly, then more and more until the children and the tree were completely surrounded.

"That's done it," groaned the boy.

"Targets for Tonight," whispered the girl.

"T-targets for T-tonight," chorused the enemy, taking careful aim.

"Jumping Jehoshophat," gasped Azdra and closed his eyes – TIGHT!

Chapter Five

Tiddledy Town

They had been airborne for some minutes before Azdra dared to open his eyes and look around. NO – it had not been his imagination – they were REALLY FLYING.

At the last moment, just before the arrows had started on their wicked way, Old Creaking Tree had made the decision of a lifetime. He was going to pull up his roots and take to the open sky. The children were caught up – one on each side – and tucked under his branches. One almighty HEAVE, and they were up, up and away.

"I say," shouted Azdra to Bel, "what a joke. We're flying through the air with the greatest of trees! In fact, he saved our lives down there."

There was no answer from Bel – only a strange, far-away look in her eyes. With the wind in her hair and her feet off the ground, she seemed to be in her element. Azdra, however, was beginning to feel sick.

"I wonder where we're going and when we'll get there?"

The answers came sooner than expected. "Oo-oh."

"Hold on to your hat!" shouted Bel, as they hurtled downwards through the night.

A few minutes later, they were on the ground, looking up, trying to catch a glimpse of their departing friend. "Old Creaking Tree doesn't beat about the bush, does he?" said Azdra. "No time for thanks or farewells or anything. I wonder if he is what they call a 'Plane' Tree?"

Bel pulled a face. "Ugh – your jokes. Where *do* they come from?"

"Out of my head, of course."

"I should have known," grinned Bel.

Azdra was walking around, peering through the gloom. "What have we fallen into this time?"

"Watch it."

"Watch it."

"Watch it," came three voices, rolling round and round his feet, "or you'll fall over the edge." The rolling voices dissolved into rolling giggles. "The edge of the table, you know. This is Tiddledly Town in Tableland and way, way down below are the Waters of Wink."

By this time Azdra was feeling quite giddy from all the comings and goings of these strange creatures.

But his eyes were getting used to the darkness, and it suddenly dawned on him that these must be the famous Tiddly Winks. He had spent many hours sitting at the table at home, trying to flip the tiny discs into a cup.

More and more winks were on the scene, rolling backwards and forwards and in and out of the children's legs, hiccupping and giggling and falling over themselves. (It must be said that the Winks loved their lemonade and suffered frequently from the rolling hiccups!)

Suddenly a cry went up. "Wink overboard! Wink overboard!"

"Help him! Help him!" shouted the Tiddly Winks, bombarding the children.

Azdra was cleaning his spectacles furiously, and trying to think at the same time. "I must have a rope and some kind of cup," he said.

"A rope and a cup to pick him up," sang the Winks as they rolled hither and thither, trying to look useful. Bel followed a yellow Wink who seemed to know where he was going, and she came back with a ball of string and a Tiddly Cup.

Then Azdra lowered the cup, tied to the string, into the waters below. And, after much splashing and three misses, finally got his man and brought him up onto the table top.

"Clever, clever, clever," sang the Tiddlies, and they rolled away to celebrate with more lemonade.

Only one wink remained – old and dirty, with very little roll left in him. Azdra's heart went out to the poor fellow. "Looks as if you could do with a bit of a lift, little one," and he put him gently into his trouser pocket.

It was getting lighter now, and time to explore the town. As the boy stretched himself, a shiver went through him and he realised how very QUIET it was. Not a giggle, not a hiccup, not a single Tiddly in sight and NO BEL. Lying on the ground was the red and white sash she had used as a sling, but – NO BEL.

He was quite ALONE! Great – he had always preferred being on his own, hadn't he? But as he slithered and ran over the flat Tableland, searching for his friend – it didn't *feel* so great any more.

On top of everything else, there hadn't been much rest for him lately, and Azdra felt tired, very tired. Still two treasures to find, he thought, and goodness only knows what was happening in Seph.

Wearily, he sat down outside a Tiddly House and SLEPT.

"Wake up, wake up. Put on your thinking cap!" Azdra was being prodded and poked in the chest. Now where had he heard that voice before? A hair tickled his nose. Squinting through half-open eyes, he saw something long, white and knotted. "Elddireth!"

"The very same – got it in one. And not without friends."

42

Looking around, Azdra met the grin of Big Tapple and the black stare of Double Six.

"Pay attention, little boy," continued the Master. "What is brown and shiny and not here?"

"Brown and shiny and – oh no," cried Azdra, feeling his shoulder. "My leather bag. You've stolen my leather bag."

"Not at all. Not at all. You shall have your bag when I have the Pearl," cackled Elddireth.

"And I have the Diamond," boomed Double Six.

"And I have the Ruby," squeaked Big Tapple.

"But..." went on Elddireth, with more menace in his voice, "unfortunately we cannot open the bag. You must undo the clasp or go back to Square One and begin again in the Land of Mog." Then he produced the bag from beneath his long, white beard.

Thank my lucky stars for a faulty clasp, thought Azdra, it's always been difficult to open. Oh my, I wish Bel was here. She would say 'Make the best use of what you have'. Well I haven't got much, that's for sure. He was feeling in his pockets for anything useful, but apart from the old Tiddly Wink and a lock of Bel's hair, the total contents were three marbles and a large safety-pin. So, they would have to do the trick.

All he wanted was a moment of confusion so that he could snatch the bag and start running. Holding up the pin, he said to Elddireth, "Here is the key we need. Come close if you please, so that I may place it in the lock."

For all his fine words, Elddireth was a man of little brain and he *did* come closer. Quick as lightning, Azdra jabbed the Master's hand with the pin and threw the marbles onto the slippery ground.

Elddireth let out a cry of pain and dropped the bag. Azdra snatched up the bag and ran. Double Six and Big Tapple tried to run after him but only ran into trouble when they slipped on the marbles and fell flat on their backs.

In and out of the houses ran Azdra, but his worries were not over. He had forgotten that Tiddledy Town was round, and that no matter how fast he ran he would still end up where he started – face to face with his enemies.

There was only one way off the table – and that was over the edge. When you gotta go, you gotta go, thought Azdra. So, holding on to his hat and his leather bag, he closed his eyes and ran…and ran… and JUMPED into the Waters of Wink.

But – "Jumping Jehoshophat!" – he had just remembered something. He couldn't swim!!

Chapter Six

Marble Mountain

Mud

The water was ICY COLD.

And Azdra felt he was swallowing most of it. Desperately splashing about with his arms and legs, he was up and down in the water like a Jack-in-the-box. Off came the spectacles, away floated Phat-in-the-hat.

"I m-must hold on. I m-must k-keep m-moving," he gurgled, bursting through the surface of the water for the third time. Gasping for air, he saw through the spray what looked like a piece of magic. His spectacles and his hat were swimming back to him – weren't they?

Something hard bumped into him, and a voice from under the hat said, "Climb on my back and we'll beat them yet."

Not stopping to ask any questions, Azdra climbed! While lying there panting and spluttering, he began to find out more about his rescuer.

He was travelling by Turtle!

And it was this Giant Turtle who was wearing his spectacles and hat! Azdra laughed with relief. But when he sat up and looked behind him he saw, to his horror, that both Double Six and Big Tapple had followed him into the water and were not far away.

The Turtle felt Azdra's fear ripple right through his shell. "Don't worry," he said softly, "they'll soon wish they'd stayed at home."

When Azdra looked again, his horror turned to amusement. Big, awkward Double Six was stuck between two rocks and Big Rosy Tapple had been captured by a seal, and was last seen bouncing up and down as the seal threw him into the air and caught him on the end of his nose.

"My friend Slippery is always willing to lend a flipper – or even a nose – when necessary," chuckled Turtle.

Tiddledly Town was now left behind, and Azdra was carried past Dartsville, round by Ludo Lake and into Chessman's Creek, to arrive weary but triumphant at…

"MARBLE MOUNTAIN," said the Turtle, like a railway station announcer, "and this is where you get off. I think you'll find it most interesting. They make very good marbles here. And I'm *told* they're bringing out a new line next week – gold marbles. What will they think of next?"

Azdra could hardly believe his luck. Was he really on the track of Gom's Gold at last? "Gosh, Turtle, I don't know how to thank you."

"Only too glad. Any friend of my cousins, the Fastoises, is a friend of mine. There is *one* thing though. I've taken rather a liking to these spectacles."

"Ah… I'm very attached to them myself, but…" Azdra hesitated. Did he really need them after all? He was beginning to see things more clearly, without them, than ever before. He made his decision and ended by saying: "Of course you can have them."

"Thanks," said the delighted Turtle. "Don't forget your hat. Good luck… and watch your step."

Azdra stood still until the Turtle was out of sight. "Now what did he mean by that, I wonder?" He turned and walked briskly away… and went knee deep into mud. Brown, bubbling mud, like a witches brew, and stretching as far as the foot of the Mountain.

Azdra retreated hastily to the water's edge. "I might have known there'd be a snag," he said, and went to push his spectacles further onto his nose – until he remembered they were on another nose now. "Oh bother!"

He found himself staring at a group of tall bamboo stems growing on the bank, and with Bel's words, 'Make use of what you have', ringing in his ears – he knew what he would do. Back home in Seph, the Stilt Bird waded through the mud on his long legs so he, Azdra, would make himself some long legs.

Using the Diamond as a knife again, he cut two of the strongest and tallest bamboos and tested them for size in the mud. When he was sure that they were both the right height, he tied a shorter bamboo to each one with tough marsh grass – these would provide the foot-rests he needed.

Getting onto the stilts was the next problem. With his back against the bank, he took hold of the poles, placed his feet on the ledges and raised himself to a standing position. The first time, he remained standing for exactly two seconds and then he was flat on his back again. But he stuck at it until he was standing long enough to enable him to start walking. Then it was time to tackle the Quaking Bog. "Are you all right up there, Phat? We've gone up in the world, did you know that?"

The walk began with difficulty and went on with difficulty. The depth of the mud kept changing and Azdra found it harder to control his home-made stilts.

To make matters worse, half-way across he was attacked by a cloud of mosquitoes. BUT – there was nothing he could do about them. He needed his hands on the stilts.

The pain from the bites on his face and hands was almost more than he could bear. Perhaps it would be easier to give up and lie down in the mud. But the thought of Seph, without leaves and without grass, made him struggle on.

"Not much further, Phat. Not much further – ooo – ooh." His voice turned into a wail as his stilts began to wobble and sway. Hidden fingers beneath the mud were pulling the bamboo sticks from side to side. Those little people of the bog – The Boggles – were up to their tricks.

"Help, help! I'm going to…" cried out Azdra, and he did. FALL! Flat – on his so sore face. But he was not going to be beaten by the mosquitoes,

by the Boggles,

or by ANYBODY.

He clawed his way through the few remaining feet of mud and collapsed, choking and panting – right in front of the entrance to Marble Mountain.

"We've – made – it – Phat," he gasped.

"NOT YET," whispered the Mountain!

Chapter Seven

Marble Mountain

2. Marbles

Someone was bumping him on the head. Azdra could hardly believe it. He was bitten and battered, dirty and splattered and now – he was being BUMPED. In between the thumps he could just make out the words, "UP, UP, UP."

"Yes, I must get up," he agreed. "But I mustn't stand before I can sit." One minute he was sitting, the next he wasn't. "What's going on round here?" asked Azdra, going down for the fourth time.

"I am…!" There was a pause in the thumping. Azdra looked up cautiously and saw that the thumper was a large, black skittle. But no ordinary skittle – this one was made of solid rubber so that he could rock and roll and twist and bend whenever the fancy took him.

"…People like you," continued Superskittle, "are always knocking me down – now you know what it's like to be on the receiving end."

"Oh, I don't *ever* want to play skittles again," said Azdra with feeling. "If only I can get into the mountain and be on my way."

"It's a deal," Superskittle looked longingly at Azdra's head, "*if* you leave your hat behind. I could do with something special to wear on Mud-days and Marble-days."

So specless and hatless – but not Phat-less – Azdra entered the mountain at last.

"WOW!" he whispered, "what a lot of marbles." And there were – piles and piles of marbles in all the colours of the paintbox; marbles in boxes, marbles in bottles (reminding him of humbugs and gob-stoppers), marbles in bags and marbles in crackers. And shaping, sorting and packing the tiny balls were hundreds of tiny Marblemen dressed in colours just as bright.

"WO – OW!" repeated Azdra, in ecstasy. There was a bouncing in his pocket. "All right, Phat. I know – we must find the GOLD."

"THE GOLD?" All the Marblemen stopped work and all of them stared at the muddy stranger. One of the men, known as M.1, jumped onto a box and looked into Azdra's eyes. "So you've heard about our NEW LINE, have you? And our secret is no secret any more. Well, well. It's no good – that Skittle will have to go."

"Oh, it wasn't Supperskittle who…"

"Never mind. You're here now and you'd better put in your orders before the rush begins," continued M.1 for all the world as if there were a queue for marbles stretching right across Quaking Bog.

Azdra was feeling the effect of the bites and bumps. And his head was aching because of the strong lights and bright colours inside the mountain – but he must GET ON. "As a matter of fact," he began, making a big effort to think clearly, "I only want *one* marble."

"Only one marble?" echoed the astonished M.1.

"*Which* one?" chorused the puzzled Marblemen.

Azdra clutched Phat in his pocket for courage. "A new GOLD one," he said.

"AH… AH," moaned the mountain.

M.1 smiled a knowing smile. "This way," he said, jumping down from the box and going towards the steps which wound round and round, up through the heart of the mountain.

Azdra followed quickly and, after him, all the little Marblemen, eager to watch the fun. Up they climbed, past the clay marbles, the glass marbles and the true marble marbles to the highest level in the factory. There – spread out before them were hundreds and hundreds of yellow balls – little stones covered in gold paint. And somewhere amongst them, only one was the PURE GOLD OF GOM.

"Jumping Jehoshophat!" cried Azdra.

"You see, my friend, what a fine display we have. If you can find the one marble you are seeking, you will be smarter than the Mighty Mog himself."

Hurriedly, Azdra opened his leather bag and picked out the Pearl of Truth and whispered:

"Pearl so true,

And Pearl so bold.

Show me the way

To the purest GOLD."

Three times, he shook the Pearl, like a dice, and threw it amongst the marbles.

The Mountain held its breath.

And the Pearl shone as it travelled in and out and over the yellow stones. Did it know the way? Would it ever stop?

It DID.

As the Pearl came to rest, Azdra, swiftly and quietly scooped up the two treasures, Truth and Power, and placed them safely in the bag.

No one spoke.

All was still.

But the Mountain was angry. So angry that it could no longer keep its anger inside. Starting from a whimper, the anger became a moan, and the moan became a rumble, and the rumble became

a roar which became

a bellow which

BURST through the

top of the Mountain. And the terrible anger took hold of Azdra. And with all its might, it hurled the boy up through the smoking crater. Away from the Low and the Master of Riddles, Double Six, and Big Tapple; away from the Giggling Winks and Superskittle, up and up on to the Faraway High.

When at last, Azdra could no longer feel the wind rushing past his ears, when his heart was no longer pounding against his ribs, when he was no longer moving – he knew that his journey had ended.

But where?

His landing had been decidedly prickly and uncomfortable, and his feet were still off the ground. In fact, he had landed in the tree in his own back yard – but not a single leaf hung from its knobbly branches.

Azdra took the bean from his pocket and watched him bouncing up and down on the palm of his hand. "Phat – oh, Phat – we're home again. In Seph! And there's Bombelina waiting for us."

All aches and pains forgotten, he scrambled down from the tree. Now that he was not wearing his spectacles, he didn't find the bird nearly as large or as terrifying as he had first thought.

"Well, Azdra," said Bombelina in that deep, dark voice, "have you anything for me?"

"Er – yes, oh yes," said Azdra. He was rummaging in his battered and dirty leather bag, and proudly produced the treasures one by one.

"Here is the Pearl of Truth, the Diamond of Strength, the Ruby of Love and HERE – is the Gold of Power."

"And..." Bombelina began.

"And...? Oh dear. I'm very sorry but I never did find the Silver of Wisdom." Phat was bouncing very excitedly in his pocket. "Phat – behave yourself," said Azdra sternly, blushing with embarrassment, and he shook his pocket roughly.

Out fell the bean and with it, the dirty old Wink he had rescued in Tiddledly Town. But the dirt had been left behind in his pocket, and the Wink wasn't a Wink at all. Azdra jumped with joy in rhythm with the bean. "Oh Phat. It was there all the time. We've done it, we've done it. We've found the Silver of Wisdom."

"Not always easy to see," said Bombelina softly. After gathering up the treasures in her beak and placing them in the silken purse around her neck, the bird looked long and hard at the boy.

"You have done a good job, Azdra, my friend, and the Great Gom is satisfied. Because you have learned to see things truly and are a little wiser, a little stronger and more loving, all will be well again in the

Land of Seph. See how the buds are swelling on the trees and the grass is turning green." And with these words, the great bird rose into the air and was gone. "Keep it green. Keep it green," came floating back on the breeze.

"I will, I will," promised Azdra, as he waved farewell. Was it his imagination or had Bombelina really winked at him before she flew away into the High?

How much he was reminded of Bel with her long black hair and strange, amber eyes! Remembering, he searched for the lock of hair which he had won in their fight over the Pearl. And he drew it from his pocket – a glossy black FEATHER.

"Jumping Jehoshophat!" he shouted, laughing. And after taking a last look at the sky, Azdra ran eagerly towards the yellow, stone house and HOME.

More Riddles From Mog

1. Why was the Leopard sad?

    Because he fell into the washing machine and came out spot-less

2. When did the Dragon-fly?

    When he saw the Sword-fish

3. Why did the U-turn?

    Because he heard the I-scream

4. Why did the Artichoke?

    Because he saw the Banana-split

Now – can you make up some riddles for yourself, using the following words?

bulrush	cloudburst
sunbeam	fingertip
jellyfish	waterfall
bluebell	paper-chase
baked beans	sugar-bowl
handshake	ballpoint